S0-BXY-431

THE TRAVELER
AND THE FLOWER

STORY BY

Mary Ann Somerville

ILLUSTRATIONS BY

Ingrid Honore

Copyright © 2012 by Mary Ann Somerville. 109721-SOME
Library of Congress Control Number: 2012902835

ISBN: Softcover   978-1-4691-6115-0
         Hardcover   978-1-4691-6116-7

All rights reserved. No part of this book may be reproduced
or transmitted in any form or by any means, electronic or
mechanical, including photocopying, recording, or by any
information storage and retrieval system, without permission
in writing from the copyright owner.

This is a work of fiction. Names, characters, places and incidents
either are the product of the author's imagination or are used
fictitiously, and any resemblance to any actual persons, living or
dead, events, or locales is entirely coincidental.

To order additional copies of this book, contact:
Xlibris Corporation
1-888-795-4274
www.Xlibris.com
Orders@Xlibris.com

This book is dedicated
with love to my beloved teacher and
friend John~Roger, who is my traveler
and the traveler in the story.

Dear Sally,

I am so happy to be getting
to know you! I hope this
next year is full of love and joy!

Love, Ingrid

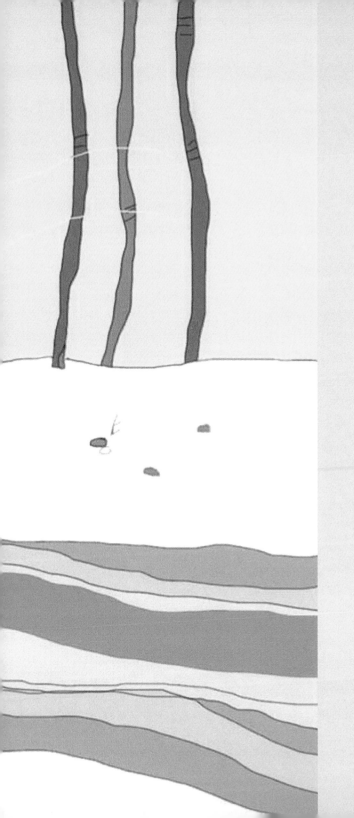

Once upon a time
in a snow covered forest
by a silver spring,
a flower was born.

At first she was only a seed buried deep
beneath the frozen earth but life breathed
within her just enough to keep her warm.

Spring was about to give birth in the forest
and so she sent forward her winds to awaken
all the living things.

The winds came in the form of gentle breezes and swept through the trees, whispering melodies of birds and love songs, rosebuds and jasmine, sweet fragrance and warmth, and they inspired all the living things to grow.

The winds swept by the silver spring and down into the dark earth where the seed was buried.

And they woke her up.

The tiny seed did not know she had been asleep until she was awakened. The sound of the wind was so beautiful and it moved so deeply within her that she decided, in that moment, that she would grow.

It took great strength, energy and courage to burst through the shell, but she did it!

Four beautiful roots stretched down into the frozen earth and a delicate green stem began to lift out of the shell, moving up and through the cold dark ground.

Now the wind left, for it was only the announcement of Spring.

The earth was still cold and the seed had to grow all the way to the top, not knowing her direction, not knowing if there was a way through the dark.

But the memory of the wind's melodies whispered in her heart and the warmth she had felt directed her.

She moved slowly, inch by inch, towards the top until one day, she broke through the earth and was greeted by a light so bright, it frightened her.

It was the sun, much warmer than the wind and more brilliant, so much so that it blinded her at first, but soon she became its friend and learned to receive from it.

And so she grew some more until one day she stood by the silver spring, a beautiful, newly formed bud with three delicate leaves, her petals just awakening in the morning dew.

It was at this time that a very wealthy man came through the forest. He was dressed in a blue robe with golden embroidery. He wore jewels on his fingers and was riding a magnificent white horse.

He came by the silver spring and stopped. Then he saw the flower.

"What a beautiful flower," he thought. "This might be the perfect flower to complete my garden."

In his most charming voice, he approached the flower and said,

"My, what a beautiful flower you are!"

(The man had learned a long time ago that a little flattery could go a long way towards getting him exactly what he wanted.)

"Little flower, I want to take you to my garden. There you will have a place designed just for you, a place which is appropriate for your beauty."

It had never occurred to the flower that she might be beautiful. She had been alone for quite a long time and was surprised by how much she was enjoying the man's attention.

So she listened as carefully as she could to everything he said and adjusted her leaves to display herself in the best way she could imagine.

The man noticed this slight change and was pleased.

"Flower," he said in an even more flattering voice, "I want to take you to my garden but first, you must unfold. I need to know that you are as beautiful as I think you are before I transport you."

The flower knew that her purpose in life was to unfold. She did not know how to unfold and she knew nothing about timing, but she decided she would try very hard to do what this fascinating man had requested.

She summoned her deepest strength, imagined herself in full bloom and did everything she could to unfold, but nothing happened.

This lack of response in the flower deeply upset the man. He was very impatient.

He wanted to see her full beauty and he had asked her very kindly, therefore she should open.

And so, (thinking if he just told her what needed correction, she would change), the man explained slowly and carefully in a rather strong voice, that her leaves were shriveled, not even close to full enough, and the petals with which she was supposed to bloom were stuffed inside her bud and that it was important and necessary that she unfold. Now!

Well, this made sense to the flower. She thought she should unfold also, especially if it meant a place in a garden designed just for her!

And so she did everything she could to unfold. She moved and she stretched, but still nothing happened.

The man took this personally. He had spent a lot of valuable time telling her what she needed to do and she did nothing.

He decided he would try force. He grabbed the flower and shook her as he said in a very loud voice,

"Flower! Unfold!"

The flower was frightened. She had never had an experience like this before. She realized that she might lose his affection and her place in his garden if she could not do what he wanted, so she tried even harder.

She pushed deep into her roots and she pushed into her leaves and she pushed into her bud with all her strength, but unfortunately she pushed so hard that she constricted the water in her stem and started to gasp for breath until her leaves drooped and even her head fell to one side.

Now this totally upset the man. He saw that she had the ability to change but she changed in the wrong direction. Angry and frustrated, he turned his back on the flower, mounted his powerful horse and left.

It wouldn't have been so bad if the flower had understood timing.

The little flower knew that her purpose in life was to unfold and she saw how much she had disappointed the man from whom she wanted affection. Feeling helpless and confused, she decided that she had failed and in this state of failure she stood, sad and alone, by the silver spring for several days.

The unfortunate thing about failure in flowers is that it prevents them from partaking of the support that is all around them.

The sun was the same and the water in the soil was the same, but the little flower had lost her courage and no longer had the will to open and receive.

Until another man came along.

This man was a traveler. He too had
journeyed through many lands, only instead
of collecting living things and objects for his
palace, he had made it his devotion to awaken
hearts.

He was a very unusual man.

He came to the silver spring for it was very
beautiful and he saw the flower and he went
over and said in a clear and gentle voice,
"My, what a beautiful flower you are!"

Now the flower had heard these words before
and wasn't particularly happy about what
might happen in this situation. She decided she
would pretend that she hadn't heard what he
said, and tried very hard to remain completely
still. However, the traveler noticed a slight
quiver in her stem.

The traveler was a very sensitive man.
He felt the little flower's sadness in his heart.

Rather than talking with her or trying to make
her feel better, he went over to the silver
spring, took the water into his own hands
and placed it gently around the base of the
flower.

The water went quickly to her roots. It was
filled with the beauty of the spring. It was
also filled with the purity of his love.

As soon as the water touched the first small
root underneath her stem she breathed it up.
She couldn't help but experience joy, so much
so that even though she still wanted to hide,
one of her leaves stretched out and her head
perked up, just a little.

The traveler was also a very wise man.

He saw these movements but decided that he would not talk with her about what to do. Instead, he sat with her by the silver spring and told her stories.

He told her of all the places he had been and of the hearts he had seen open and of the wondrous people who had shown him the beauty of his own heart. He also told her that everything would be all right. He taught her about time and how every flower will unfold, but timing is the key.

As he told her these stories, the flower relaxed and as she relaxed, she began to blossom.

The traveler also taught her things. He taught her that if she reached, not pushed, but reached towards the sun, she could receive more. If she opened her leaves in a certain way, she could gather the sun in every pore and hold the dew as nourishment.

And, every day, he brought her water from the spring and laid it at the base of her stem until one day the beautiful white flower blossomed.

She stood by the silver spring, a radiant and beautiful flower, her petals fully open, glistening in the warmth of the morning sun.

It was at this moment that the little flower knew she had fulfilled her purpose and it was at this moment that she knew the traveler would leave.

But you see, something wonderful had happened.

The little flower's roots were now strong and deep. She could reach to the spring by herself and she was gathering the water on her own.

Her blossoms were so soft and beautiful that she felt total joy in sharing her beauty with the forest and by giving, she fully opened and received.

And so, the traveler and the flower parted in great understanding and joy.

* * * * * * * * * *

Now, some people say that the flower would have bloomed anyway and that the traveler didn't make any difference.

But you see, I saw the flower.

I saw the caring of the traveler and the radiance that blossomed.

And, it is my belief that the flower was a perfect gift from the traveler to the forest.

With special thanks to my mother, Annabelle Phillips Dickey who taught me the healing power of stories and to Berti Klein, Joey Hubbard, Alex Padilla and Jane Cremer who encouraged me to share my stories.

I also want to express my deepest love and gratitude to John-Roger, my spiritual teacher, friend and traveler and to John Morton, who has been my friend and traveler many times when I did not know how to unfold.

And, appreciation beyond words to Ingrid Honore, the illustrator of this story. I met Ingrid in a completely unexpected way and she has been a gift to me, creating pictures for the story that are more beautiful than I could have imagined.

As the story foretold, life has a way of unfolding perfectly, if we will allow ourselves to relax and enjoy God's perfect timing.

MARY ANN SOMERVILLE M.S.S. is an international consultant, seminar leader and executive coach devoted to the heart wisdom in all people. This story is in honor of all the people she has met and the courageous beauty with which they express their hearts' purpose. Mary Ann is also a minister in the Movement of Spiritual Inner Awareness, a non-denominational church teaching the principles of soul transcendence.

INGRID HONORE is a self-taught artist who is known for her unique vision and ability as a painter, illustrator and musician. She is a collector of all things unusual and interesting...beach rocks, blue jars and bottles, succulents, tea cups, antique clothing and anything with unicorns. She lives in Santa Barbara with her beautiful young daughter, a source of inspiration and joy.

Edwards Brothers Malloy
Thorofare, NJ USA
November 26, 2012